Tim and Tooth Fairy

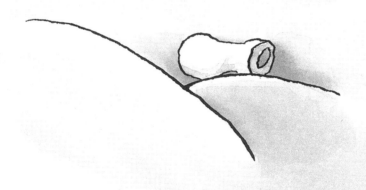

Celia Warren
Illustrated by Judy Brown

Beth had a wobbly tooth.
It had wobbled and wobbled for weeks.

2

One day, Beth bit into
a big red apple.
Her wobbly tooth
came out.

"Wow!" said Beth.
"Now the tooth fairy
will come, and I will
get a coin."

3

At bedtime, Beth put the tooth
under her pillow and went to sleep.

The next morning, Beth looked under
her pillow.
The tooth was gone and in its place,
there was a shiny coin.

"I've got a coin!" said Beth.

"The tooth fairy gave me a coin!"

"I want a coin, too," said Tim.

"Your teeth aren't wobbly yet," said Mum.

All day, Tim pushed and pulled his teeth,
but not one tooth was wobbly.

Tim had an idea.

He got out his modelling clay and made a toy tooth.

"I'll put this under my pillow," he said.

"Then the tooth fairy will come and give me a coin."

"The tooth fairy only takes real teeth,"
said Beth.
"She won't give you a coin for a toy tooth."
"Yes, she will," said Tim.

At bedtime, Tim put the toy tooth
under his pillow.
He went to sleep and dreamed
about the tooth fairy.

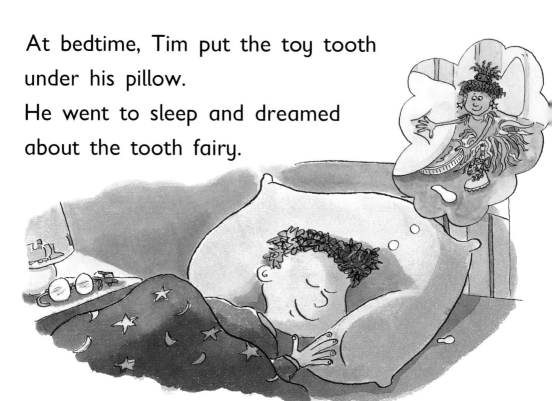

Beth couldn't sleep.
She knew the tooth fairy
wouldn't come and Tim would
be upset in the morning.

Beth went downstairs to see Mum.

She told Mum about the toy tooth.

"The tooth fairy won't come, will she, Mum?"
said Beth.

"Let's wait and see," said Mum.

The next morning, Tim jumped on
Beth's bed.
"Beth! Look! I got a coin!
The tooth fairy did come!" he said.

"Let me see," said Beth.

Beth looked at the coin.

It wasn't a real coin, it was a toy coin,

but she didn't tell Tim that.

Tim ran to Mum.

"Mum! Mum! I got a coin from the tooth fairy," he said.

"I want to go to the shop now."

"You can't go to the shop with that coin,"
said Mum.
"You see, it's a toy coin.
You gave the tooth fairy a toy tooth,
so she gave you a toy coin."

Tim looked sad.

Then Beth had an idea.

"You can come to my shop," she said.

"What would you like to buy?"

"I'd like a big red apple, please," said Tim.

"To make my real tooth come out."